The Stalker

GAIL ANDERSON-DARGATZ

The Stalker

Grass Roots Press

The Good Reads series is funded in part by the Government of Canada's Office of Literacy and Essential Skills.

Grass Roots Press also gratefully acknowledges the financial support for its publishing programs provided by the following agencies: the Government of Canada through the Canada Book Fund and the Government of Alberta through the Alberta Foundation for the Arts.

Grass Roots Press would also like to thank ABC Life Literacy Canada for their support. Good Reads® is used under licence from ABC Life Literacy Canada.

Library and Archives Canada Cataloguing in Publication

Anderson-Dargatz, Gail, 1963–
    The stalker / Gail Anderson-Dargatz.

(Good reads series)
ISBN 978-1-926583-29-7

    1. Readers for new literates. I. Title. II. Series: Good reads series (Edmonton, Alta.)

PS8551.N3574S72 2010   428.6'2   C2010–901987–3

Printed and bound in Canada.

| Distributed to libraries and educational and community organizations by **Grass Roots Press** www.grassrootsbooks.net | Distributed to retail outlets by **HarperCollins Canada Ltd.** www.harpercollins.ca |

For Irene Anderson

Chapter One

The stalker phoned me for the first time early on a Saturday morning. The ringing of my cell phone woke me. I grabbed the phone from the nightstand and flipped it open.

"Hello?"

"Hello, Mike," the guy on the other end said. He sounded like one of those space aliens from the TV show *Stargate SG-1*, the ones with glowing eyes. The caller's strange, deep voice told me that he had voice-changing software on his phone, but I felt sure I was talking to a man.

"Nice day for a little kayak trip, eh?" he said. "But I wouldn't go out if I were you."

"Who is this?"

The guy hung up. I checked the list of callers on my phone, but there was no caller ID. No name, no number.

"Nut case," I said aloud. "Thanks for waking me up." Then I glanced at the clock. Five-thirty. I had to get up anyway.

I run sea kayak tours. My staff and I guide tourists as they paddle my boats around the many islands along the coast of Vancouver Island. I have ten kayaks, each paddled by one person.

The summer when I got that weird phone call, I had three employees. They only worked for me during the spring and summer, in the tourist season. Jason led the one-day kayak tours around the local bay. I took clients on weekend or week-long wilderness adventures. Each of us had an assistant guide. This person helped with the tour and also had first aid training.

On the longer trips, my assistant guide was also a cook. Without those great meals, the tourists simply wouldn't come back. Sara had been my cook and assistant for five years, ever since I started my business. But Sara's husband didn't like her being away so much in the summer. So, to make him happy, she told me she would work only the one-day tours with Jason. That's when I hired Liz to cook and be my assistant guide on those longer trips.

The morning I got that phone call, Liz had been working for me for about a month. She was a great cook and easy to get along with. I liked her. But that was it. I never got involved with the women who worked for me. That would just be asking for trouble.

Still, no one can blame a guy for looking. And Liz was a pleasure to look at. She was fit from so much kayaking, and she rode her bicycle almost all year. She was a natural beauty.

My business is very small. I attract most of my clients with my website and by word of mouth, and my kitchen is my office. At six-thirty that morning, I looked up from my coffee, and there Liz was, framed by the window of my kitchen door. She usually kept her long brown hair pulled back in a ponytail. But not this morning. Her hair was loose around her shoulders. She wore a pink tank top, one of those tight ones with skinny straps, and no bra underneath.

"Hello, Mike," she said when I opened the door.

"Liz! What are you doing here? I thought we were supposed to meet at the marina."

I never meet clients at my house. Instead, I load enough kayaks for the trip on my trailer, hitch it to my truck, and drive to the town marina. I meet my clients there, and then we drive together to the starting point for the tour. The marina is a natural place to meet because it's the only real tourist attraction in this town.

"So far, you've been late for every one of our trips," Liz said. "I stand there waiting with the clients, making up excuses for you." She twirled her hair with one finger and grinned. "I thought I would make sure you were on time for a change."

"This is the west coast," I said. "No one is ever on time."

Liz stepped inside carrying her "dry bag." This waterproof bag held the change of clothes she'd need if she got wet. Her "dry suit," her waterproof pants and shirt, were slung over one arm. We would both put on these dry suits when we reached our launching place. We had to keep warm and dry as we paddled along the coast. The kayaks sat so low in the water that we often got splashed by waves or spray from the paddles. Storms often hit without much warning, too.

Liz lived just down the road from me. That's how I'd ended up hiring her. I had met her at the mailboxes on the corner. She was looking for work just when Sara said she wanted to switch to the one-day tours. Even better, Liz was a trained cook. In fact, she had owned her own café in Port Alberni until the economy tanked.

"Need help loading?" Liz asked. She pointed at my Ford pickup.

I shook my head. "No. We're all set to go."

I had already loaded the truck with the food and gear for that weekend's tour, and the kayaks were on the trailer. Our group would fit into the pickup's crew cab. There would be only four of us on this trip: me, Liz, and two guys from Vancouver. Their company developed computer programs that made maps. In short, the clients were a couple of computer geeks.

I hadn't talked to either of them yet. All I knew were their names: Gerald Williams and Sam Andrews. A secretary had booked their tour. She told me that their boss had decided to send them on this trip. They didn't get along, and their dislike of each other was bad for business. The boss hoped they would get to know each other better on the kayak tour. He thought a "bonding experience" would stop their arguing.

"Are you ready for this?" Liz asked. I had told her what we were getting into.

"No," I said. Fortunately, the trip wasn't one of my week-long tours. I just had to get through today, and we would head home Sunday afternoon. Besides, the company that had sent these two clients my way had paid me very well. I had explained that I charged per person. Taking only two people out for the weekend wasn't cost effective. The company had agreed to pay the bill for the eight-person tour I usually ran.

"What's with the tank top?" I asked Liz. "I haven't seen you dress like that before."

She looked down. "You don't like it?"

I shrugged. "You don't strike me as a tank top kind of gal."

I felt sorry as soon as the words came out of my mouth. The tank top did suit her. I couldn't keep my eyes off it, or her. That was the problem.

Liz, hurt, turned away. "Can I use your washroom to change my shirt before we head out?" she said quietly.

"Sure."

She carried her dry bag into the washroom. I took a sip from my coffee and tried to come up with some way to say I was sorry without making things worse. Then my cell phone rang. I pulled it from my pocket and answered it.

"Liz is there, isn't she?" The caller was the man with the space-alien voice who had woken me up an hour before. He knew who Liz was, and he had to be close, watching my house. I pulled back the kitchen curtain to look out the window. The street was quiet. Most folks were still sleeping on this Saturday morning.

"Where are you?" I said. "How did you get this number?" Not even my mother had my cell phone number. She called me on my home phone. I had given my cell phone number to my employees and to my clients, but not to anyone else. I hadn't even listed it on my company's website.

"I know she's there," the voice said. "I saw her go inside."

"Who is this?" I said.

"I'm watching you," the guy said. "Stay home."

Chapter Two

Liz and I met our tour group down at the marina. Artists' studios, cafés, and a fish and chips shop lined the waterfront. Fishermen's boats were tied up along the docks beside the tourists' sailboats and motorboats. Across the inlet, mist drifted down the rocky cliffs. The scene was postcard perfect.

Jason was already there, as we had arranged. He sat at a table outside the donut shop with a balding man and a middle-aged woman. Jason would drive with us out to the launch site, and then he would drive my truck back to town. The next day, he would pick us up farther along the coast. That way, the clients didn't have to paddle back.

"You're late," Jason said as Liz and I reached his table. Other than the strange fact that he was always on time, he was a real west-coast guy. He wore sandals year round, though in the winter he wore wool socks with them. When he wasn't guiding kayak tours for me, he played his guitar at the marina. He set his open guitar case on the sidewalk beside him, and tourists threw money into it. Busking paid well for him because he was a talented musician.

I ignored him and held out my hand to the man seated next to him. "I'm Mike, your guide for the weekend. And this is our other guide, and your chef, Liz."

The man stood and took Liz's hand first. He actually kissed it. "A real pleasure to meet you," he said. Then he went on holding her hand as he gazed into her eyes. Liz pulled her hand away and laughed nervously.

"I've never had a man kiss my hand before," she said.

"Yeah, he's a real charmer," said the woman seated beside him. Her sour face showed that she believed otherwise.

"Gerald Williams," the man said when he shook my hand. "I'm so looking forward to this." He had a thick, lisping, upper-crust English accent. In fact, his accent was so pronounced that I wondered if he was faking it.

"Have you just recently moved to Canada?" I asked him.

"Hell, no," the woman said. "He's lived in Vancouver for twenty-five years. The accent comes and goes, depending on who he's trying to impress."

I assumed by the way she talked about Gerald that this woman was his wife. I guessed she was here to see him off, but he hadn't introduced her. That seemed odd. Also, I caught her checking me out in a way most wives wouldn't, at least not in front of their husbands. She looked at me so long that I wondered for a moment if there was something wrong with my face or hair.

I took a quick look at my reflection in the donut shop window. Everything seemed in order. Sara had told me I had "rugged good looks." I guess she was right. I have a strong nose and a square jaw. I only shave every couple of days, so I often have a chin full of stubble, as I did this day. One of the benefits of running a kayak tour business is that I stay fit. My high school buddies had already started to grow beer-bellies, but I had gained nothing but muscle.

"Are we still waiting for our other guest?" I asked Jason.

"I am your other guest," the woman said. She held out her hand. "Samantha Andrews."

"Oh, I'm sorry, Samantha." I said. "When the secretary told me your company would send two computer experts and their names were Gerald and Sam —"

"I know," she said. "You assumed we were both men. Surprise, surprise."

"You don't have to make a federal case out of it," Gerald told her. "He made an honest mistake."

I felt an instant dislike for Gerald, so I hated to agree with him. But almost anyone would think at first that someone named "Sam" was a man. Samantha was right about one thing, though. Gerald's heavy English accent did come and go. I noticed only a hint of it when he talked to her.

"Men always underestimate what women can do," she said. "They hear the title 'doctor' or 'computer programmer,' and they assume the person must be a man."

"Oh, here we go," said Gerald. "Another lecture from Sam."

"That's Samantha to you," she said. Samantha turned away and drank coffee from one of the donut shop's mugs. Her short hair was carefully styled and stiff with hairspray. She wore a dry suit that she had obviously bought especially for this trip. The plastic loop that once held the price tag was still on her sleeve.

Gerald hadn't bought his coffee here at the donut shop. His throw-away cup and his box of donuts came from Tim Hortons. He held up his coffee when he saw me glance at it. "Will there be a Tim Hortons anywhere along our route?" he asked.

Jason snorted out a laugh.

"No," I said. "I'm afraid not."

"No coffee shops of any kind," said Jason. "No nothing, for miles and miles."

Jason was right. We were about to kayak along some of Vancouver Island's most rugged and isolated shores. We likely wouldn't see another soul for the two days.

"I wish I'd known," Gerald said. "I would have brought a thermos."

"I'll make you coffee," said Liz.

"That's reassuring," said Samantha. "I suppose we'll all sit around a fire and drink it out of tin cups. Are we going to sing camp songs, too?" Samantha clearly did not want to be there.

"Oh, give it up," said Gerald. "What could be more fun that wandering the Canadian wilderness in a canoe?"

"Kayak," Samantha said, correcting him.

"Kayak, canoe," Gerald said. "What's the difference? A boat is a boat."

"Actually, there are quite a few differences between a kayak and a canoe," I said. "For one thing, the paddler of a canoe either sits on a seat or kneels. When you go out today in your kayak, you'll sit with your legs stretched out in front of you. Also, you'll use a kayak paddle that has a blade on each end. In other words, you'll use both ends of your paddle to move the kayak along, first one end and then the other.

Canoe paddles have a handgrip at one end and a blade at the other."

"Oh, look, look!" Gerald cried. I doubt he'd taken in a word I said. He waved at a totem pole down by the waterfront. "I love this stuff," he said. "Here, take a picture of me beside it, will you?" He handed his camera to me and trotted over to the totem pole, expecting me to follow. "I've got a collection of Indian baskets and cutting tools at home," he said. "I try to pick up something every time I leave the city."

I did take my clients to ancient First Nations sites. I had planned to show Gerald and Samantha a burial site in a cave that day. But removing anything from these sites was against the law. I knew right then that Gerald would cause me a whole lot of trouble.

Chapter Three

As I handed Gerald his camera back, who should drive into the parking lot but Sara. She had two kayaks and her gear in the back of her pickup. Now that she worked on the one-day trips with Jason instead of coming on the longer trips with me, I was surprised to see her.

"What are you doing here?" I asked her. "This is your day off."

"You're not planning to come with us, are you?" Liz nodded at the kayaks in Sara's truck.

"Oh, no," said Sara. "Dave and I are going out for an hour or two later."

"Is Dave with you?" I asked Sara. The rising sun hit the windshield of her truck, so I couldn't see whether her husband was there or not. I hoped he wasn't. He was jealous, even though nothing had ever gone on between Sara and me. Sara and Dave had argued before nearly every one of the tours she and I had taken together. He didn't want her to go. Dave said Sara gave me way more time than she gave him during the summer, and he was right. Every year, we spent several weeks together, guiding tours. Now, of course, all that had changed.

Sara shook her head. "He's still in bed, sleeping. I'll pick him up later."

"And get changed, I expect," said Liz. She nodded at Sara's short dress and then glanced at me. Clearly, she still felt hurt by the comment I had made about her tank top that morning.

Sara glanced down at her dress but said nothing. The two women eyed each other for a moment.

Sara looked good that morning. Her blond hair was loose around her shoulders. She wore plenty of makeup, which she never did when she helped me with kayak tours. And her swingy little summer dress showed a whole lot of thigh. I had never seen her in a dress before.

I introduced her to our clients. "This is Sara, one of our guides," I said. "Sara, this is Gerald and Samantha."

"Call me Sam," said Samantha. "All my friends do."

Gerald rolled his eyes.

"Sam it is," I said.

After Sara had greeted them, both Gerald and Sam started text messaging, typing on their phones with their thumbs. I had the feeling that neither of them would be much fun.

Jason finished loading the clients' gear into my truck and joined us. "Just can't stay away from us, eh?" he said to Sara.

Sara shrugged. "I guess I miss going out there with you," she said. As she spoke, she looked at me and not at Jason. "Anyway, what is a kayak tour without these?" She handed me a plastic bag full of her wonderful oatmeal raisin cookies. They were still warm and smelled of cinnamon. She had brought along a bag of these cookies on nearly every tour we did together.

"Thanks," I said. "For the clients?"

"For you," Sara said. "They were always for you." Her smile took my breath away.

Liz cleared her throat. "Ready to go?" she asked me.

"Yes, yes of course," I said. "All right, everyone. Let's head out."

"Will we get cell phone reception out there?" Gerald asked.

"Absolutely," said Jason. "We count on it in case of emergencies."

That pulled Sam's attention away from texting on her phone. "Emergencies?"

"We've never had one in five years," I said, trying to reassure her. "But of course we have to be prepared."

"Prepared for what, exactly?" she said.

"This is the west coast," said Jason. "We have to be prepared for anything." He winked at Sam and she turned pale.

"We're not likely to run into any killer whales, are we?" she asked.

"Orcas?" said Jason. "Yes, there's a good chance you'll see a pod." That was true. We were likely to see a group of these beautiful black and white whales. They might even swim along beside our kayaks.

"They don't eat humans, right?" asked Gerald.

"We're not a staple in their diet," said Jason. "But we would make a good snack, don't you think?"

I gave Jason a hard look to get him to shut up. The last thing we needed was to make Sam and Gerald more nervous than they already were. "Orca attacks on humans are very rare," I said. "And orcas tend to attack only when they are captive in marine parks. You will be perfectly safe. I'll make sure of it."

Gerald didn't look convinced. "So you *can* guarantee cell phone reception," he said.

Jason shook his head. "We can't *guarantee* anything. Most of the time we have reception, but like I said, this is the west coast. Phone reception sometimes cuts out around the back sides of the islands. And if a storm comes up —"

"I doubt we'll have a problem," I said quickly, and I nudged Jason. He had a habit of saying far too much.

"I better make a call before we leave," Gerald said. He walked over to the grassy area by the children's playground, dialling his cell phone as he went.

"And I better go home," said Sara. She turned before reaching her truck. "I'll make sure Jason remembers to pick you up tomorrow."

I watched Sara get in her truck. She was so lovely, and after five years of running kayak tours with her I figured I knew her better than anyone. She was the closest thing I had to a best friend. Like her, I missed our time together.

As Sara drove off, my cell phone rang. The caller was the guy with the strange alien voice. "I know where you're going," he said. "You go and I'll be out on the water with you."

I held the phone against my chest. "Jason, are you playing one of your sick jokes on me?" I asked.

Jason held up both hands. "What?" He wasn't using his cell phone.

"Never mind." I put the phone back to my ear.

"This is no joke," the guy said. "I know where you're going. I can see you right now."

I looked around the marina. There was the fish and chip shop, the tiny artists' studios lined up one beside the other, the empty picnic tables, and the children's playground. I noticed a guy sitting in a pickup truck down the road, but I couldn't tell if he was on the phone or not. Liz and Sam were out of view, waiting behind my truck. Gerald was still on his cell phone. Surely Gerald wasn't the creep talking to me now? Gerald saw me looking at him and raised his hand as if he thought I had asked him to hurry up. Then he turned his back on me to finish his call.

"You've been warned," the voice said. "Don't go out on the water."

Was it Gerald? The weird voice on my cell didn't carry even a hint of an English accent. But then Gerald's accent came and went. But why would Gerald try to freak me out? I didn't even know him.

"Who is this? What do you want?" Maybe it *was* the guy in the truck. When I walked towards the truck to see if the driver was in fact on the phone, he drove off.

"Go home," the caller said.

"Stop phoning," I said. "I'll track your number, find out who you are, and call the cops."

Actually, I had no idea how to find out this guy's phone number. He must have blocked it, because it didn't show up on my phone display or call history list. In any case, my threat didn't scare him off.

"You go out," he said, "and people will get hurt."

Chapter Four

We all squeezed into my truck. I drove, and Liz sat between Jason and me in the front seat. Sam and Gerald sat in the crew cab behind us. As we started the drive to our launch site, I could see Sam in the rear-view mirror. She was eyeing Jason. "What exactly did you mean earlier?" she asked him. "You said on the west coast we have to be prepared for anything."

Jason shrugged. "Just what I said. Out here we learn to expect the unexpected."

"Like what?"

"Like that tourist who went missing a while back," Jason said.

"They don't need to hear that story," I said.

"Yes we do," Sam and Gerald said at the same time. In the rear-view mirror, I saw them scowl at each other. They were like a couple of bickering kids.

I gave Jason a warning glance. "They don't need to hear that story," I said again.

But Jason ignored me. "This tourist went out kayaking alone," he said. "No guide. Then a couple of fishermen found his boat just barely afloat. The kayak was full of bullet holes. And the guy's gun was inside. A few days later, his body was found."

"Suicide?" Sam asked.

"No bullet wounds on him," said Jason. "He had drowned. The thing is, his backpack was still in that kayak, filled with arrowheads, beads, cutting tools, and several animal skulls."

Gerald looked at first alarmed and then elated. "Indian artifacts?" he asked.

"Very likely taken from a First Nations burial cave," I said. "There used to be several skeletons in one of the caves I took clients to. Now there's nothing in that cave."

Gerald sat on the edge of his seat, leaning over my shoulder. I could smell the coffee on his breath. "People are allowed to take things from these caves?" He sounded far too excited.

"Absolutely not," I said. "Taking things from those sites is illegal."

He sat back in his seat, clearly disappointed.

"Tourists steal things from these sites and get away with it all the time," said Liz. "The items rarely get back to the bands they belong to."

"Indian bands, you mean?" asked Gerald.

"The First Nations communities," I said. "The families the items belonged to. And around here we use the term First Nations, not Indian."

"Ah."

Liz turned to look Gerald in the eye. "How would you feel if your grandmother's grave was dug up? What if some guy took her wedding ring or even her bones home as a souvenir?"

I nudged Liz with my elbow. I didn't like this guy much, either, but I couldn't afford to lose clients or have them badmouth my company when they got home.

"The location of these burial caves is all hush-hush now," Jason said. "We're not supposed to know where most of them are."

I caught Jason's eye and shook my head, but he didn't catch on. I didn't want Gerald to get any ideas. I wouldn't be taking him or any other client to the hidden caves. But Jason kept on talking. "In fact, there are islands that don't appear on maps," he said. "These islands have sacred sites on them that the government and the First Nations don't want anyone to know about."

Gerald sat forward again. "Really?" he said. "There are still arrowheads and tools on these islands? Oh, you're going to have to take me to some." When his eyes met mine in the mirror, he added. "I just want to locate them with my GPS."

"I'm sorry," I said. "That won't be possible." There was no way I would let this guy use his electronic mapping toy to record where these sacred sites were. Lord knows what he would do with that information. He might add the locations to maps on the internet. Before long, tourists even more thoughtless than he was could disturb the burial caves. "We are allowed to take you to the cave you'll see today," I said, glancing back at Gerald. "But no others."

"Allowed?" he said. "By who?"

"We have the permission of the band."

Gerald put a hand on my shoulder. "But you know of other burial caves, right?" he said. "Caves no one is supposed to know about? Caves other tourists may not have seen or disturbed?"

I wished to god Jason hadn't opened his big mouth. "Yes," I said. "But we're not going there."

"I could make it worth your while." When I raised an eyebrow to Gerald in the rear-view mirror, he added, "I promise I won't take anything."

Bullshit, I thought. "That's out of the question. I have to stay on good terms with the band."

Gerald was pissed. He sat in the seat behind us, pouting. "I came on this tour to see Indian artifacts," he said. "And I want to see an undisturbed site."

"Oh, no," said Sam. "We both know you're here to make nice-nice with me."

Gerald grunted and crossed his arms. He and Sam stared out their separate windows.

Jason attempted to joke Gerald out of his funk. "You wouldn't want to end up with bullet holes in your kayak, would you?"

I held up my hand. "There was no evidence of foul play in that tourist's death. The authorities said he drowned and closed the case. Who knows? The guy may have committed suicide for all we know."

"Yeah," said Jason. "To kill himself, he first loaded his kayak with things from a sacred site. Then he shot holes into his kayak to sink it. You know what I think?" he asked, as if that wasn't already obvious. He turned and looked back at Gerald over his shoulder. "I think some local got fed up with tourists messing with the burial grounds."

"You mean someone from the Indian — er, First Nations — band," said Sam.

I had to stop such dangerous guessing. "If it was someone from the band," I said, "then he would have taken those items back to the grave."

"Unless he wanted to send a message," said Jason. "Maybe he wanted to warn tourists to stay the hell away from the burial caves."

"Then why would the murderer try to get rid of the evidence?" I asked. "Remember, it looked as if someone had tried to sink the kayak with the things from the burial site still inside. There were all those bullet holes in the hull."

That stumped Jason.

No one knew what had really happened to that tourist. His death simply didn't make sense. But the conversation got me thinking. Tourists trespassed so often on the sacred sites that some band members wanted to ban kayak tours altogether. The guy who had phoned me that morning had told me to stay home, to stay off the water. Was he warning me to stay away from the burial caves?

Chapter Five

At the launch site, Jason and I carried the four kayaks down to the beach. Liz started unloading our gear from the truck. Gerald ate his donuts and watched us work. Sam stood beside him with her arms crossed. She wouldn't help us, either. At one point, I saw Gerald offer Sam one of his donuts. She took it. Progress, I thought. We were only an hour into our trip, and they were already starting to bond.

Liz loaded her dry bag and the bags of food into her own kayak, pushing them under the enclosed front and back ends of the boat. I had learned that Liz liked to do things her own way. There was hell to pay if Jason loaded her kayak and she later found her food supplies damaged.

We said our goodbyes to Jason and put on our life jackets. Liz and I stood in shallow water as we held the kayaks steady for our clients. I helped Gerald and Liz helped Sam climb into their boats. We told them to sit just to the rear of the cockpit, placing their feet inside. Then, using their arms for support, they slid their behinds down onto the cockpit seat and stretched their legs out in front of them.

Once we were all in our kayaks and on the water, I taught them how to paddle. They each held the paddle in the middle, gripping it with both hands. Then they dipped first one end and then the other into the water. As they pulled each blade back through the water, they propelled their boats forward. Paddle on the left, then paddle on the right. Once they felt safe doing this, I taught them different paddle strokes that would help them steer. Then we were away.

But after less than a half-hour of paddling, Gerald's cell phone rang. "All right!" he said. "We're still getting reception."

Gerald stopped paddling to take the call and fell behind. I slowed my paddling so I didn't get too far ahead of him as Liz continued on with

Sam. I would have to talk to Gerald when he got off the phone. If he took a call every ten minutes we'd never get anywhere.

Then my own cell phone rang. I looked for a number before answering, but there wasn't one. "Hello," I said, expecting the worst, and I got it.

"Turn around and go home," the space-alien voice said.

"Screw you," I said.

"I can see you. I can see that Liz and the other woman are far ahead of you."

I looked around at the string of islands ahead of us and at the shore. The mist was heavy along the shoreline, but as far as I could tell, there was no one out here but our little group. Jason had driven away long ago. I couldn't hear what Gerald said as he talked on his cell phone, but he had to be my caller. There was no one else around.

"I can see that bald guy talking on the phone," the voice said. "I can see you looking at him."

So the creep wasn't Gerald. Or was it? Gerald could be trying to make me think it wasn't him.

"If you value your life, you'll turn around," the guy said. Then he hung up.

I tucked the phone back in the pocket of my dry suit and ran a hand over my mouth. Gerald was still talking on the phone. Up ahead, Liz and Sam had stopped paddling as Liz answered her phone and began to talk. Sam immediately took out her own cell and started text messaging. After a moment, Liz turned in her kayak and, still on her phone, waved for me to catch up.

"Gerald," I called. "We've got to go. We won't reach that burial cave before dark at this rate."

"All right, all right," he called back. I waited until he caught up with me and then we paddled to catch up with Liz and Sam.

Liz signalled for me to hang back as Gerald and Sam paddled on ahead. "We've got a situation," she said when they were out of earshot.

"You got a call from some creep, right?"

"He's been phoning you, too?"

"I got several calls this morning. Was this your first?"

"Uh-huh. No name, no number."

"Yeah, he must have a block on it."

"He said he can see us, Mike. He's got to be watching from the shore somewhere."

"Or he's with us." I looked ahead at our two computer experts.

"Gerald?" said Liz.

"He was on the phone just now. And he was on the phone back at the marina when I got one of the calls. No one else was."

"What's your history with him?" she asked me.

"I don't have a history. I didn't meet him until this morning. But who else could it be?"

"Sam started texting after I answered my phone," said Liz. "So I think we can rule her out."

"In any case, it was a man's voice."

"That doesn't mean much these days. Anyone can download software off the internet to change his or her voice. And the voice of this caller was certainly changed."

"What did he say to you?"

"To turn back," she said. "To go home. He said I didn't belong here."

"Then maybe Gerald isn't the stalker," I said. "He wants to be out here, to see those caves."

"The caller could just be playing a prank, right?" Liz said. "Jason does this kind of thing, doesn't he? Didn't he put a garter snake in your kayak once?"

"Yeah. Another time it was a squirrel," I said. "Halfway to Cedar Island, I felt it crawling up my leg. Very funny." I didn't tell her I had screamed like a girl. "But the stalker isn't Jason. He wasn't on the phone when I got one of the calls."

"What if he got one of his friends to do it? Remember, in the truck, Jason made a point of telling that story about the tourist found dead. He tried to scare us."

"I don't know," I said. "This isn't like Jason. I think we should call the cops."

Liz shook her head. "They won't do much until the stalker threatens to hurt us."

"He did. He said someone would get hurt if we came out here."

"You can trace the call," said Liz. "The telephone company will make a note of the number of the last call made to your phone. Their staff will hand that number over to the police. But the operator won't tell you who the caller was. At least, that's how it all works on my home phone."

"How do you know?"

She paused for a moment. "My ex-husband stalked me after we split up. I finally had to get a restraining order to stop him. He's not allowed to phone me or come near me. He knows he'll be arrested if he does."

"Oh, god, I'm so sorry."

"It's over now."

"Or is it?" I said. I held up my cell phone. "Could this guy be your ex-husband?"

She looked out over the misty shore for a moment before answering. "I don't know. Maybe."

"I saw a guy sitting in his truck down at the marina. He drove off when I walked towards him."

"What did he look like?" Liz asked.

"I don't know. He was too far away for me to see his face."

Liz shook her head. "I thought this was all over." Then she looked at me. "I'll tell you one thing. No matter who this guy is, I'm not going to let a stalker run my life ever again."

"So what do you want to do?" I asked her.

"We stick to our plans. We take Sam and Gerald to the burial cave. I'll make a nice dinner. And we'll see what happens. First, let's watch to see if Gerald is on the phone when we get the next call."

"And if he is?"

"I guess we'll just have to confront him, as politely as we can. Ask him what the hell he's up to."

"And what if he isn't on the phone when we get the next call?"

Liz scanned the wilderness around us. "Then we have a much bigger problem on our hands."

Chapter Six

For the next couple of hours, Gerald stopped paddling every fifteen minutes or so to check where we were on his GPS. "Gerald," I said finally, "we'll never get to that cave if you keep stopping. And look at those storm clouds. We'll have to find a place to camp soon."

"Storm?" Sam looked up at the boiling clouds above us. "My god! Where did that come from?"

"They roll up quickly here," I said. Most of my clients lacked the experience to paddle in rough water. When storms hit, we had to make camp on one of the islands. There we would wait until the storm passed.

Gerald didn't hear a word. He puzzled over his GPS unit, then waved excitedly at the island to our left. The rocky shore shot up into a cliff that was full of shallow caves. Bone Island, we called it. We often paddled by, but we never went to shore.

"That island doesn't appear on the map," Gerald said. He held up his GPS unit. "Look! Here we are." He showed me a blip on the screen. "And here is where that island should be. But there's nothing on the map but water. That's one of the forbidden islands, isn't it?"

I glanced at Liz. "The burial cave I'm taking you to is on an island up ahead."

"But I want to go there," he said, pointing again at Bone Island.

"No," I said. "We aren't allowed."

"I knew it! That is one of the forbidden islands." And Gerald was off, paddling towards Bone Island.

"Gerald!" I called. "You can't go there!"

But Gerald didn't turn back. I paddled after him. I caught up to him easily, but how could I get him to turn around? If I grabbed him, I risked overturning his kayak.

I pulled ahead and crossed his path to make him turn. "Listen to me, Gerald," I said. "You can't go on that island. Taking things from these sites is illegal. You could be charged."

"I just want to look," he said. But his childish whine told me he lied. He wanted a souvenir.

"We're turning around," I said.

"No."

"There is plenty to see in the cave I'll show you," I told him.

"But I want to see those caves," he said, pointing at Bone Island directly ahead of us. Many of the caves were burial caves, and they contained human remains and the items buried with them. We were almost to shore.

"Shit," I said. We would have to beach before I could talk some sense into him. And even then, I figured, I would need Sam's help. She knew the guy. I turned and waved at the women, inviting them to meet us on the beach of Bone Island.

We dragged our kayaks on shore, one by one. Together with Liz, Sam and I tried to talk some sense into Gerald. But then Sam's phone rang. She listened to the caller for a moment and said, "Who is this?" Then she held the phone away from her ear. "What the hell? He hung up on me."

"Who?" Gerald asked.

"I don't know," said Sam. "His voice was very strange."

"Like a space alien's voice?" I asked.

"How did you know?"

So Gerald wasn't the stalker. He hadn't been on the phone when Sam got the call.

"What did the caller say?" Liz asked Sam.

"He said we don't belong here. Then he said people would get hurt if we didn't turn around and go home."

Liz and I both nodded.

"This guy has phoned you, too?" asked Sam.

"A couple of times when we were out on the water," I said. I hesitated. "And a few times just before we left."

"And you took us out into this godforsaken wilderness anyway?" said Sam.

I wouldn't tell them I thought the caller was Gerald. And I wouldn't tell them about Liz's ex, not unless I had to. "We thought maybe it was just one of Jason's pranks," I said.

"A prank?" said Sam.

"He put a snake in my kayak once," I said.

"Then a squirrel," Liz added.

"I got him back by letting a tarantula loose in his bedroom," I said. Liz and I both tried to laugh.

"Is this the humour you Canadians are so famous for?" Gerald said. "If so, I don't find it very funny."

I shook my head. "Me neither. Look, why don't I phone Jason right now and find out if it is him. Then we don't have to worry."

I pushed my speed dial button to get Jason. He answered with his usual clipped greeting: "Hey." But I could barely hear him. His voice kept cutting in and out as we spoke. The storm was affecting cell phone reception. A few drops of rain had already fallen.

"Have you been making prank calls to us?" I said. "Threatening us? They've got to stop."

"You know I wouldn't do anything like that," said Jason.

I paused before saying anything more. I did know, of course. "I'm sorry," I said. "Things are kind of crazy right now."

"What's going on?"

"We're on Bone Island. Some creep is out here with us, watching. He's been making calls to Liz and me and now to Sam. He threatened us."

"Oh, man," Jason said. "You *are* coming home, right?"

I looked up at the boiling clouds above us. The rain hammered down now. "Yeah," I said. "It'll be tough paddling for Gerald and Sam but I think we better give it a try. If we run into trouble, we'll find a place to wait out this storm. I'll call you once we get close to the launch site. You can meet us there."

"I'll wait for your call, then."

"Thanks, buddy." I flipped my phone shut. "All right, everyone. Let's go."

"But I haven't seen the burial caves," said Gerald. "And I'm not leaving until I do." He climbed up the rocky beach in the rain, sliding on the slick rocks that led up to the closest cave.

"Ah, hell," I said. I climbed up after him, leaping from rock to rock. When I put a hand on his shoulder, he shrugged it off.

"Are you going to knock me out and drag me back down this cliff?" he said. "If not, I suggest you allow me to see that cave. I'm not leaving here until I do."

"All right, all right," I said. "We'll *all* go together and see *one* of the burial caves." The more eyes on Gerald the better, I thought. "Then we're getting out of here. Agreed?"

"Agreed."

I waved at Liz and Sam to join us. We all climbed the cliff with our hoods up, braving the heavy rain. We balanced along a thin ledge under a long, narrow rock overhang to view the grave.

Gerald was disappointed. He looked into the grave glumly, like a child who has just dropped his ice cream. The cave was shallow, little more than a pocket in the cliff face. The remains of a body were still in there. The skeleton was partly covered by the rotted cedar burial box that had once contained it. If the cave had ever held anything else, it had long since been taken away.

"That's it?" said Gerald.

"Well, what did you expect?" said Sam. "King Tut's tomb?"

"I think it's amazing," said Liz. "I know we're not supposed to be here, Mike, but thanks for this." She squeezed my hand.

"Now," I said. "Let's go."

But as we turned to take our first step back down the cliff, gunshots zinged past our heads.

Chapter Seven

The gunman fired down from the cliff edge above us. Because of the narrow overhang, he couldn't actually hit us. But the bullets were close. I heard the zing as one flew just in front of our faces. We all pressed ourselves against the cliff face as the shots rained down.

"Did you see him?" said Liz.

I shook my head. "No."

"Why is he shooting at us?" asked Gerald.

"That's obvious: he doesn't want us here," I said. "He's trying to scare us off."

"Someone from the Indian band?" Gerald asked.

"I don't know," I said. But likely he was right. The stalker had warned us not to come out here, and then he shot at us when we intruded on this cave.

"We should just leave," said Sam. "Run down to shore and get in our kayaks."

"Not with this guy shooting at us," I said.

"What, then?" she said. "We're trapped."

I flipped open my phone. "I'll call the cops." But I got no signal.

"Must be the storm," Liz said. "I'll try." She tried her phone, then shook her head.

Sam and Gerald both pulled out their cell phones. "Nothing," said Sam.

"Well, at least we won't get any more calls from that stalker," I said, trying to make light of the situation. Nobody laughed.

The shots stopped for a moment. The guy needed to reload his gun, I thought. I squinted up into the rain to see if I could catch sight of him, but I couldn't. "You want us to leave, we'll leave," I shouted up at him. "Just stop shooting."

Immediately the guy started firing again. I jumped back under the overhang. But this time he didn't aim at us. He shot at our kayaks. One by one, the boats jumped as he shot them full of bullet holes. Then the shots stopped. We all listened to the pouring rain, waiting for the gunfire to start again.

"Oh, god," said Liz. "Now we really are trapped. We can't get off the island."

Sam's voice rose in alarm. "He shot holes in our kayaks, and now he's going to kill us, like he killed that tourist!"

"We can't afford to panic," I said. "So far he seems more intent on scaring us than killing us."

"What are we going to do?" said Gerald.

"What can we do?" Liz said. "We wait this guy out. And we wait this storm out." She pointed at the shallow caves in the cliff wall on either side of us. "We can hide here."

"At least that way he'll have to show his face if he plans to kill us," said Sam. She was right. The cliff was a natural fortress. The stalker would have to stand on shore or climb up the rocks below us if he intended to shoot us. We would see him coming.

"All right," I said, taking charge. "Each of these caves is big enough for only one of us, so I'll give you each a cave."

"I'm not going into a cave with a body," said Sam.

"There are several here without remains," I said. "Stay in there, keep your head low. We'll just wait it out, like Liz says. As soon as the storm lets up and our phones work, I'll call for help."

I led Sam and Gerald along the cave face under the overhang. I chose caves for each of them that had boulders in front of them. These rocks would provide at least some protection if the gunman decided to fire directly at us. Gerald's cave was little more than a shallow dent in the rock face. But it was fairly dry, and it held nothing for him to steal.

When Gerald saw the cave was empty, he backed out and said, far too loudly, "But I want to see the other burial caves."

I pushed him into his cave. I feared that the stalker might take another shot at him for that one. "Look, asshole," I said. "You dragged us here and got us shot at. For your own safety, you will shut up and do what I say for the rest of the trip. Understand?"

As Gerald nodded, rain dripped from his hair. "I understand."

Sam, listening from her own cave, began to clap. Quietly at first, then in real applause.

That night, I kept watch from my little cave. My jackknife stayed in my hand, open and ready. The rain didn't let up. The wind howled eerily across the mouths of the burial caves above and around us. Sometime in the night, I heard footsteps outside my cave. My heart beating hard in my chest, I sat up too quickly and jabbed myself in the shoulder with my own knife. I pressed my hand against the small wound, feeling the blood slick on my fingers. "Who's there?" I said. "I can hear you."

"It's just me." Liz appeared in the cave entrance. She carried the tiny flashlight she kept in her dry suit. Her hair was completely wet from the rain. She looked helpless, beautiful.

"Can I double up with you tonight?" she asked. When I didn't answer immediately, she said, "I'm not here for *that*."

"I didn't think you were."

"I'm just so scared and cold."

I closed up the jackknife and shifted over to give her room. The cave was barely big enough for one person, let alone two. We had to lie curled up together on our sides to fit. Liz lay with her back to me. She smelled clean, of Ivory soap and rain. I liked her for that.

"You can feel the spirits of the dead all around us," Liz said. "The stalker is right. We don't belong here. What are we doing bringing tourists to these graveyards?"

"We don't know for sure the gunman is from the band," I said. "The guy could be your ex, for all we know."

"Thanks for that cheerful thought," she said.

"I'm sorry," I said. "Being trapped here is frightening for all of us, but it must be so much more terrifying for you. You went through all this before, with your ex-husband."

"He didn't try to shoot me."

"But I get the idea that he threatened you."

"Yes, many times."

We both listened to the storm raging outside.

"I meant to apologize earlier for what I said about your top this morning." I said. "I was out of line."

"No, you were right," she said. "What I wore wasn't appropriate."

"Well, it did make me uncomfortable."

"I shouldn't have worn it."

"No. I mean, I liked it. You looked nice. That was what made me uncomfortable."

She turned to face me. Our noses were only inches apart. "I wore it for you," she said.

I grinned. "Then I hope you wear it again sometime."

"I'll think about it."

I could hear a smile in her voice. I leaned forward and kissed her in the dark. But she turned away as best she could in the cramped cave.

"I'm sorry," I said. "I thought that's what you wanted."

She shook her head. "You like Sara."

"She's married."

"She likes you."

I thought about Sara's dress, the cookies she had brought me, the way she had smiled at me that morning. "She knows I don't get involved with my employees," I said. "Besides, I would never break up a marriage."

"But if Dave wasn't in the way…"

"But he is in the way. I'm not interested in getting involved with Sara."

"Because she's married."

"Yes, because she's married."

That didn't seem to be enough for Liz. "And you don't get involved with your employees," she said. "I'm an employee."

"Fine," I said. "Let's just forget that kiss ever happened."

But after a time she backed up against me and I wrapped an arm around her. We didn't make love or even kiss, but I held her body close to mine.

"Do you think the stalker is still out there?" Liz asked.

I paused a moment before responding. I wanted to reassure her, to make her feel safe. But I knew that, somewhere out there, a guy with a gun waited for us to come out.

"I don't know," I said.

Chapter Eight

As daylight came, the storm started to move on. But I still had no phone reception. Perhaps the cliff itself blocked the signal. Even so, there was no way I was going to step down onto the beach to check. The stalker might still be waiting with his gun on the cliff above us. One shot and it would be game over for me.

Then I heard the sound of a motorboat heading our way. I climbed over Liz, waking her. "What?" she said, still half asleep. "What is it?"

"A boat," I said. "Someone's here."

When I peeked over the rocky ledge in front of my cave, I saw Sara jumping to the shore from my motorboat. She tied the boat to a driftwood log. Jason leapt out of the boat after her. I stood up, pressing my body against the cliff face, and called their names, waving my arms.

Sara waved back until she saw Liz come out of the cave behind me. She let her arm fall.

"Is everyone all right?" Jason called up to us. "You had me scared shitless. You phone to tell us some guy is threatening you, you say you're coming home, and that's the last I hear from you."

I looked back to the caves. Sam poked her head out of hers. Gerald stood up and stretched. "Yeah, I guess we're all right," I said. "But check out the kayaks." Gunshot holes peppered the boat hulls.

"Oh, my god," said Sara. "You're living that missing tourist story all over again."

"The guy shot directly at us, too, from up there." I pointed at the top of the cliff above me. "He had us trapped in these caves all night."

"I don't see anyone up there now," Jason said. "I think it's safe to come down."

We all scrambled down the rocks to shore. Despite our dry suits, we were wet, cold, and shivering. Sam and Gerald both went directly to their kayaks, looking for a change of clothes.

"I'll fire up my camp stove," said Liz. "Make us coffee and something to eat to warm us up."

I hugged Sara and slapped Jason on the shoulder. "I can't tell you how glad I am to see you two," I said.

"When you didn't call or turn up at the launch site," Jason said, "I tried to phone you. But I couldn't reach you. I phoned Sara, and at last I got hold of her. I wanted to come out here late last night. But Sara convinced me that the water was just too rough. So we waited out the storm. I'm kicking myself now. We got plenty of rain, all right, but Sara and I could have made it out. That gunman could have killed you."

"It's all right," I said. "I understand."

"What are you doing on this island, anyway?" asked Jason. "You know it's off limits."

"Oh, I know, all right," I said. When I looked back at Gerald, he slunk off behind a bush to change his pants.

"Hey!" cried Liz. "Orcas!" We all watched the huge, majestic creatures roll through the waves as they swam between Bone Island and the shore of Vancouver Island. Liz was spellbound. Her hair blew around her face as she watched the pod pass. I had never seen a sight more beautiful than Liz watching the orcas.

"I really do miss this," said Sara. "Being out here. With you."

Sara turned to me, but my focus was on Liz. Sara held up her cell phone in front of me. "I've been getting those calls, too," she said.

That got my attention. "What did the guy say?"

"He threatened me," Sara said. "He said he knows about you and me."

"You and me?" I led Sara away, so Liz, Jason, and the others couldn't hear. "Listen," I said. "Is there any chance the caller, the stalker, might be your husband? You said he was jealous of our trips together, of you and me."

"Dave?" Sara laughed. "I wish he cared enough to do something like this. Hell, he doesn't even buy me flowers on our anniversary."

"I'm sorry I suggested it," I said. "I just wish to hell I knew who this guy was."

"It's pretty clear he's trying to scare you away from these sacred sites. For your own safety, I would listen if I were you. Why not just run the day trips around the bay with me? You can sleep at home every night."

"No. I'm getting the cops involved. I'm not going to let this stalker ruin my business."

As if on cue, my cell phone rang. I opened my phone as I scanned the bush along shore and the cliff above us. Was the stalker that close, I wondered, that he could hear our conversation?

"Mike?" The caller was a man, but he wasn't the stalker. At least his voice wasn't bent out of shape by voice-changing software.

"This is Dave," the caller said. "Sara's husband. Have you seen Sara? She told me she was staying overnight at her sister's place. I tried to reach her on her cell phone early this morning. When she didn't answer, I phoned her sister. Jenny told me Sara hadn't stayed there last night. I tried phoning you earlier, too, but I couldn't reach you."

Suddenly everything fell into place. Sam had hit the nail on the head yesterday: men always underestimate what women can do. I felt like the guy in the movie *Fatal Attraction*, stalked by a sick woman. And that woman was Sara. The stalker had to be her. She knew not only my cell phone number and Liz's, but my clients' as well. She knew our tour route, where we were going.

Sara must have shot those holes in the kayaks to keep us here on Bone Island and then kayaked home. She was a strong kayaker, nearly as strong as me. She could have weathered the storm, no problem. Then she would be nowhere near Bone Island in the morning. No one would suspect that she was the stalker. After all, she met Jason at the launch site so they could come out here. The one thing she hadn't counted on was her husband's phone calls. First to her sister, and then to me.

I looked right at Sara as I answered Dave. "Sara's here, on Bone Island, with Jason and Liz and me."

Sara stared back at me for a moment. She knew her husband was on the phone. She knew she had been caught. She knew I had figured out that she was the stalker.

Sara walked away from me, back to my motorboat. I started to follow, with my phone still at my ear. I wouldn't let her take off with my boat, leaving us stranded on this island.

"Bone Island?" said Dave. "What the hell is she doing out there? For that matter, what are you doing there? I thought no one was allowed on Bone Island."

Sara climbed into the boat. But then she jumped right back out again, carrying her backpack. There was something odd about the way Sara marched towards Liz and the others, who all stood around the camp stove. She was too determined. Her head was down, like a bull's when it's ready to charge.

"Let me talk to her, will you?" said Dave.

"I'll have her phone you back," I said.

"Tell her she has me really worried."

Me too, I thought, as I closed my phone.

"What's up?" Jason asked Sara when she reached them.

"This," said Sara. She pulled a handgun from her backpack and pointed it straight at Liz's head. Liz looked up from the omelette she was cooking, more surprised than frightened. But Sam screamed.

"Sara, put the gun down," I said. But Sara stepped forward and pressed the gun against Liz's forehead. Liz slowly placed the omelette pan on the ground beside her and held her hands in the air.

"Wait," I said to Sara. "I understand. You shot those holes in the kayaks to scare me, so I wouldn't bring clients out here again. So I wouldn't come out with Liz again. I get it. You don't have to shoot Liz to get her out of the picture. I doubt that she wants to work for me after this."

"*This* is our stalker?" Gerald asked.

"*You* shot those holes in the kayaks?" Sam said. "Whatever were you thinking? We nearly died of exposure in those wretched caves."

Sara levelled the gun at Sam and then Gerald. "Shut up," she said. "Both of you, shut up." Sam and Gerald each took a step back and didn't say another word. Sara's hand shook as she turned the gun back to Liz's forehead.

"She thinks she can just come in here, take over, take you from me," Sara said to me.

"She couldn't take me away," I said. "I thought you and I were good friends. That would never change."

"We spent five years together out on the water, and you wouldn't touch me. She works for you for just a few weeks, and there she is, sleeping in that cave with you."

"You're married," I said. "Dave loves you. He wants to be with you. He's worried about you."

She aimed the gun at me. She was in tears. "But *I* love *you*," she said.

"Believe me," Liz said. "This isn't love."

Sara swung the gun back to Liz. "Be quiet!" she cried.

I saw the tension ripple through Sara's forearm and her finger start to squeeze the trigger. I didn't think, I just reacted. I grabbed the gun from Sara's hand as she fired. A bullet whizzed past Liz's ear and nearly hit Sam.

I threw the gun to the ground. Sara stared at it a moment. We all stared at it. Then Sara took off down the beach. I chased after her and grabbed her arm to stop her. She tried to pull away, but I held her from behind as she struggled and cried out. After a time, she gave up. Her shoulders shook as she sobbed in my arms. She leaned her head back against my shoulder.

"I just wanted you to love me," she said. "The way I love you."

I looked back at Liz and the others standing around the camp stove, watching us. "Liz is right," I said. "This isn't love."

Chapter Nine

Back home the next morning, I woke to a weird buzzing sound. I thought for a moment that a large, panicked beetle was trying to get out my bedroom window. Then I watched my cell phone vibrate right across my nightstand and fall to the carpet. I had turned the ringer off. I didn't ever want to hear that thing ring again.

I reached down and grabbed the phone from the floor.

"Hello?" My voice was still thick with sleep.

"Did I wake you?" The caller was Liz.

I turned the alarm clock to face me. "I guess I slept in. But then, it *is* my day off."

"I feel stupid now. I just assumed you'd be awake."

I sat up in bed and rubbed my face. "What's up?"

"This can wait."

"Tell me," I said.

"Did you hear any more from the cops about Sara?"

"No, not really. I guess both you and I will have to appear in court sometime."

"Yeah, sounds like it."

"Sara's husband phoned, though," I said.

"Aw, hell. I thought he might."

"He wanted to know if I saw any warning signs in Sara's behaviour before she flipped out. He asked if Sara and I were having an affair."

"Were you?" Liz asked.

"No!" I said. "She flirted with me, I guess. But I thought we were just friends. I still can't believe she was the stalker."

"Before our divorce, I never would have believed my ex was capable of what he did."

Neither of us said anything for a moment.

"You didn't phone to ask about Sara, did you?" I said, finally.

"Not really. But that can wait for another time."

"Come on."

She paused. "I wanted to talk about what happened in the cave on Bone Island Saturday night."

"You were scared. I understand. Forget it ever happened."

"I'm not sure I want to forget it," she said.

Now I paused, long enough that Liz asked, "You still there?"

"I do make it a policy not to get involved with my employees," I said. "Seems like a good rule, after this past weekend."

"I understand." She sounded hurt.

I got out of bed. "However, we could come up with a different arrangement. You could run your own catering and guiding business. I could hire your company to cook for my tours and help with guiding. That way, our companies would work together, not you and me personally. Strictly speaking, you wouldn't be my employee."

Liz didn't say anything at first. Through the phone, I heard what I thought were footsteps and then the slam of a truck door. Was she starting up her truck? I went to the kitchen in my T-shirt and jockey shorts to look out my window at her house. Sure enough, she was in her truck.

"Funny you should mention that," she said. "I've decided to start my own business. I quit. Now, are you interested in a contract with Liz's Catering and Guiding Company? I'm good with a paddle, and I make a mean western omelette." She did make the best western omelettes. Her secret ingredient was sausage, farmer's sausage instead of ham.

"I think we can come to some agreement," I said.

"Then Sunday was officially my last day," she said.

"I usually ask for two weeks' notice before I let an employee quit. In your case, I could overlook that. *If* you deliver your letter of resignation *in person*."

There was another long pause. I watched her drive her truck into my yard, get out, and jog up my path. And there she was, framed in the window of the kitchen door, wearing that tight little pink tank top, her hair loose around her shoulders. Her cell phone was pressed to her ear. "I'll be right there," she said, and she closed her phone.

Acknowledgements

Many thanks to Laurel Boone for her careful edits of this novel. Thanks also to Chris Wood, whose story "On a Misty Sea, a Dark Discovery" appeared in the online publication *The Tyee*. The real-life event reported in that story inspired the conversation in chapter four about the tourist who drowned. Lastly, thanks to all the many tourists who enjoy the wilderness areas of the BC coast responsibly and leave it as they found it.

Good **Reads**

Discover Canada's Bestselling Authors with Good Reads Books

Good Reads authors have a special talent—
the ability to tell a great story, using clear language.

Good Reads books are ideal for people

❋ on the go, who want a short read;

❋ who want to experience the joy of reading;

❋ who want to get into the reading habit.

To find out more, please visit
www.GoodReadsBooks.com

The Good Reads project is sponsored by
ABC Life Literacy Canada.

The project is funded in part by the Government of Canada's
Office of Literacy and Essential Skills.

Libraries and literacy and education markets
order from Grass Roots Press.

Bookstores and other retail outlets order from HarperCollins Canada.

Good Reads Series

If you enjoyed this Good Reads book,
you can find more at your local library or bookstore.

2010

The Stalker by Gail Anderson-Dargatz
In From the Cold by Deborah Ellis
Shipwreck by Maureen Jennings
The Picture of Nobody by Rabindranath Maharaj
The Hangman by Louise Penny
Easy Money by Gail Vaz-Oxlade

2011 Authors

Joseph Boyden
Marina Endicott
Joy Fielding
Robert Hough
Anthony Hyde
Frances Itani

For more information on Good Reads,
visit **www.GoodReadsBooks.com**

The Picture of Nobody

by Rabindranath Maharaj

Tommy lives with his family in Ajax, a small town close to Toronto. His parents are Ismaili Muslims who immigrated to Canada before Tommy was born. Tommy, a shy, chubby seventeen-year-old, feels like an outsider.

The arrest of a terrorist group in Toronto turns Tommy's world upside down. No one noticed him before. Now, he experiences the sting of racism at the local coffee shop where he works part-time. A group of young men who hang out at the coffee shop begin to bully him. In spite, Tommy commits an act of revenge against the group's ringleader.

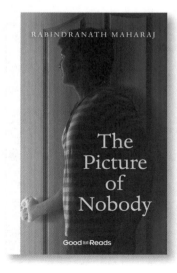

Shipwreck
by Maureen Jennings

A retired police detective tells a story from his family's history. This is his story…

On a cold winter morning in 1873, a crowd gathers on the shore of a Nova Scotia fishing village. A stormy sea has thrown a ship onto the rocks. The villagers work bravely to save the ship's crew. But many die.

When young Will Murdoch and the local priest examine the bodies, they discover gold and diamonds. They suspect that the shipwreck

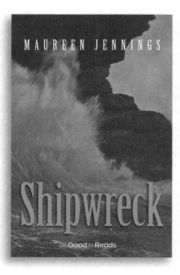

was not responsible for all of the deaths. With the priest's help, Will—who grows up to be a famous detective— solves his first mystery.

The Hangman

by Louise Penny

On a cold November morning, a jogger runs through the woods in the peaceful Quebec village of Three Pines. On his run, he finds a dead man hanging from a tree.

The dead man was a guest at the local Inn and Spa. He might have been looking for peace and quiet, but something else found him. Something horrible.

Did the man take his own life? Or was he murdered? Chief Inspector Armand Gamache is called to the crime scene. As Gamache follows the trail of clues, he opens a door into the past. And he learns the true reason why the man came to Three Pines.

In From the Cold
by Deborah Ellis

Rose and her daughter Hazel are on the run in a big city. During the day, Rose and Hazel live in a shack hidden in the bushes. At night, they look for food in garbage bins.

In the summer, living in the shack was like an adventure for Hazel. But now, winter is coming and the nights are cold.

Hazel is starting to miss her friends and her school. Rose is trying to do the right thing for her daughter, but everything is going so wrong. Will Hazel stay loyal to her mother, or will she try to return to her old life?

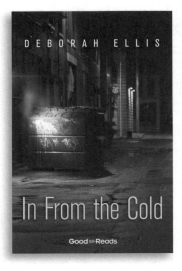

Easy Money

by Gail Vaz-Oxlade

Wish you could find a money book that doesn't make your eyes glaze over or your brain hurt? Easy Money is for you.

Gail knows you work hard for your money, so in her usual honest and practical style she will show you how to make your money work for you. Budgeting, saving, and getting your debt paid off have never been so easy to understand or to do. Follow Gail's plan and take control of your money.

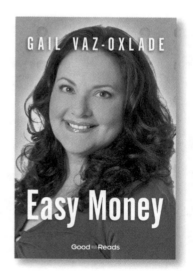

About the Author

 MITCH KRUPP

Gail Anderson-Dargatz is the author of the bestselling novels *A Recipe for Bees* and *The Cure for Death by Lightning*, both finalists for the Giller Prize. She currently teaches fiction in the creative writing program at the University of British Columbia. Gail lives with her husband and children in the Shuswap region of BC, the landscape found in so much of her writing.

Also by Gail Anderson-Dargatz:

The Miss Hereford Stories
The Cure for Death by Lightning
A Recipe for Bees
A Rhinestone Button
Turtle Valley

You can visit Gail's website at
www.gailanderson-dargatz.ca